Freight Train
Donald Crews

Greenwillow Books

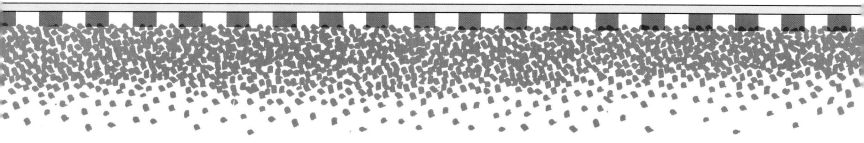

Library of Congress Cataloging in Publication Data. Crews, Donald. Freight Train. "Greenwillow Books."
Summary: Brief text and illustrations trace the journey of a colorful train as it goes through tunnels, by cities, and
over trestles. [1. Railroads—Trains—Pictorial works. 2. Colors. 3. Picture books]   I. Title.   PZ7.C8682Fr
[E] 78-2303   ISBN 0-688-80165-X (trade) ISBN 0-688-84165-1 (lib. bdg.) ISBN 0-688-11701-5 (pbk.)

With due respect to Casey Jones, John Henry, The Rock Island Line, and the countless freight trains passed and passing the big house in Cottondale

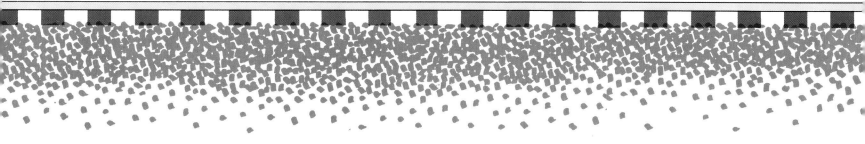

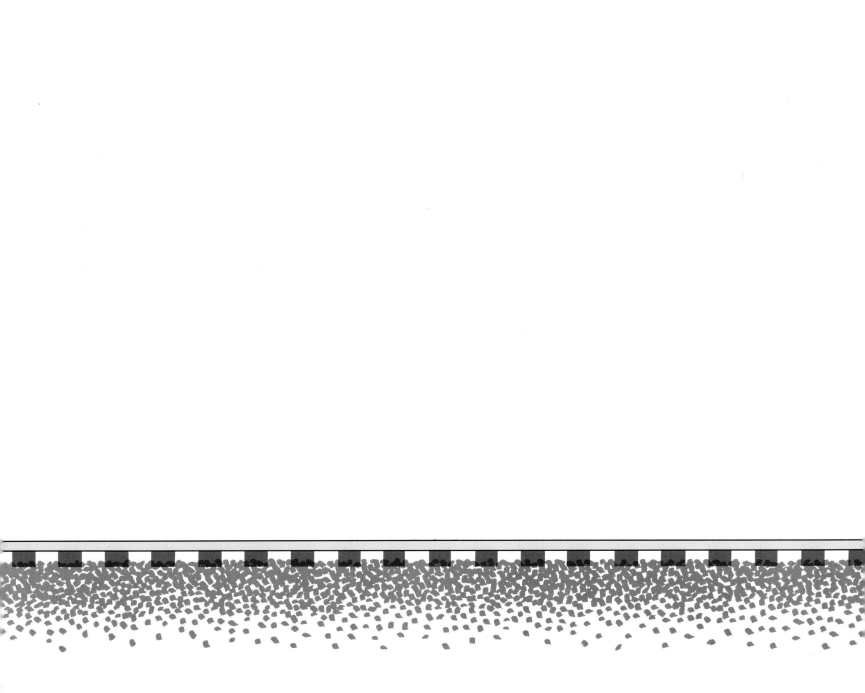

A train runs across this track.

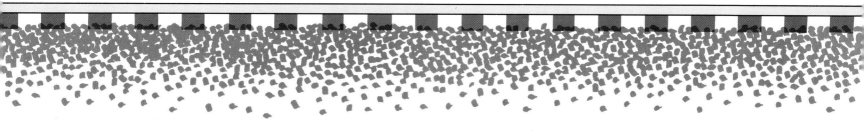

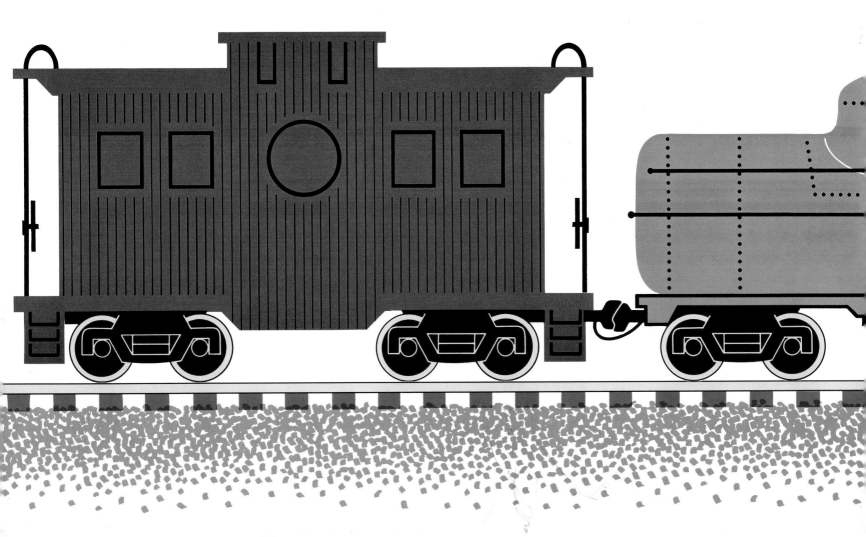

Red caboose at the back

Orange tank car next

Yellow
hopper car

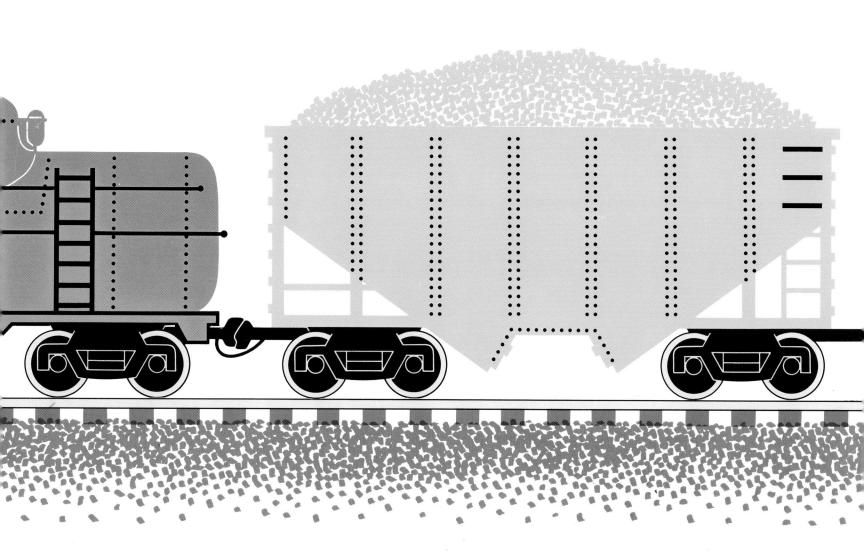

Green cattle car

Blue gondola car

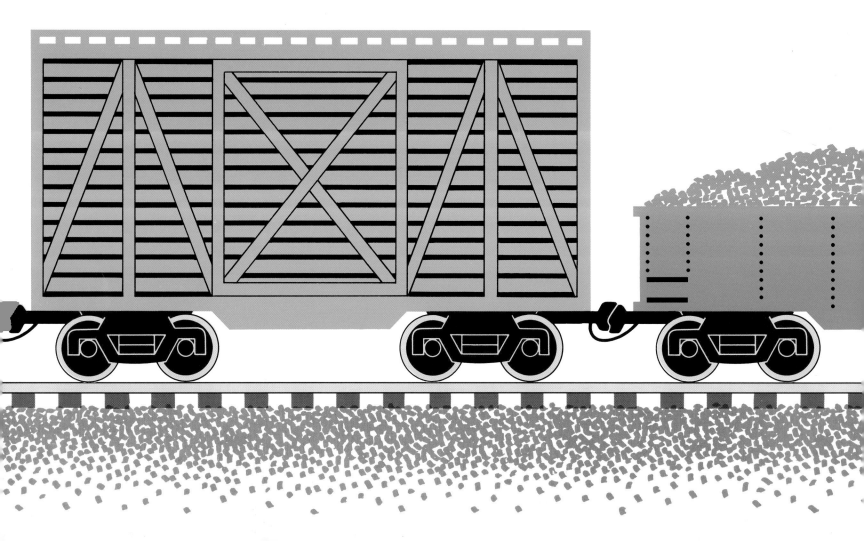

Purple
box car

a Black tender and

a Black
steam engine.

N&A

Freight train.

Moving.

Going through tunnels

Going by cities

Crossing trestles.

Moving in darkness.

Moving in daylight. Going, going...

gone.

DATE DUE
